Timeless Fairy Tales

Snow White
and the Seven Dwarfs

AWARD PUBLICATIONS LIMITED

In the heart of a forest stood an old castle. In the castle lived a king and queen. They had a lovely baby daughter called Snow White, but the Queen was always anxious about her. One day, as the Queen was sewing a dress for Snow White, she pricked her finger with the needle. As the Queen looked at the drop of blood on her finger she made a wish.

"May our daughter Snow White grow into a beautiful child. May her hair be as dark as a raven, and her skin be as white as snow."

Snow White did indeed grow into a lovely child, but sadly, the Queen died when Snow White was still very young.

Later, the King married again. The new Queen was beautiful, but vain. She was also wicked, and had once been a witch. She had a magic mirror which she often asked:

"Mirror, mirror, on the wall, who is the fairest of us all?"

The mirror always answered, "You are fairest, my Queen."

One day the Queen asked the mirror, "Who is the fairest of us all?"

The mirror answered, "Snow White is fairest of you all."

At first the Queen couldn't believe what she had heard, but the mirror repeated, "Snow White is fairest of you all."

The wicked Queen was very angry.

In a rage, she ordered a woodcutter to take Snow White into the forest and kill her.

Fortunately, the woodcutter was a kind man. He had no wish to harm a hair on Snow White's lovely head. So he told Snow White to run away and hide from the wicked Queen, and never to go near the palace again.

After saying goodbye to the woodcutter, Snow White walked through the forest. She walked and walked until she was a long way from the castle.

On her journey she made friends with the animals. The birds brought her berries and nuts to eat. But as the day wore on, Snow White grew worried. She didn't know where she was going to shelter for the night.

As it grew dark, Snow White felt very tired. She was just about to lie down beneath a tree, when she came upon a tiny cottage, almost hidden under a hawthorn tree.

Snow White went up the short path to the tiny cottage, and knocked on the front door. In her hand she carried a gift of flowers from the forest.

When no one answered, Snow White opened the door and stepped inside. She entered a small room.

Around the table were seven little chairs and stools. Upon the table were seven little cups. "Who can live here?" wondered Snow White.

Snow White wanted to sit down, but most of the chairs seemed too small. She didn't know what to do. So she went into another room and found a small bed.

"I do hope no one will mind if I lie down here," she said. She didn't know that the little cottage belonged to seven dwarfs.

As she lay on the bed, some of her animal friends came to keep her company. Very soon, Snow White was fast asleep.

The dwarfs had been hard at work all day, mining gold in the secret mountains. As Snow White slept, they were marching home for tea.

The dwarfs were friendly with the animals, but when a rabbit came to tell them that they had a visitor called Princess Snow White, the dwarfs didn't believe him.

When the dwarfs arrived back at their cottage in the forest they had a great surprise. The rabbit had been telling the truth. They did have a visitor, and her skin was white as snow.

The dwarfs just stood and stared at the beautiful Princess. For a time no one spoke.

Snow White began to wake. "I must be dreaming!" she cried as she opened her eyes and saw the dwarfs standing there.

"Don't be afraid," said the eldest dwarf. "We will not harm you. Tell us what has brought you to our home in the forest, and we will try to help you."

"I am a Princess," explained Snow White, "but my stepmother wants to kill me! I walked through the forest all day looking for somewhere to rest and finally found your cottage. Please will you help me?"

"You must be Princess Snow White!" said one of the dwarfs. "Don't worry. We will shelter you from the wicked Queen, and take care of you."

The seven dwarfs built a chair and bed specially
for Snow White and brought her little gifts carved
from wood and stone. In the evenings they all sat by
the fireside and the dwarfs told stories.

In return for their kindness, Snow White cooked
for them and kept their cottage clean and tidy.

After a time, Snow White forgot her fear of the
wicked Queen.

A month passed. Then one day, when Snow White was alone in the cottage, who should come creeping through the woods, but the wicked Queen. Once again, she had asked the magic mirror who was the fairest. When it had replied, "Snow White is fairest," the jealous Queen knew that Snow White was still alive.

As the Queen passed through the forest, even the trees looked unhappy. Animals fled in fear. Some animals tried to warn Snow White, but the wicked Queen stopped them in their tracks using her powerful magic.

The wicked Queen came to Snow White's window disguised as an old woman, carrying a basket full of ribbons.

"Here's a pretty ribbon for your dress," she called to Snow White. "Come out and let me tie it for you."

"You're very kind," smiled Snow White, "but I am afraid I can't afford to buy a ribbon."

"You may have the ribbon as a gift," insisted the wicked Queen. "I have plenty of them."

"Thank you," smiled Snow White. "The red ribbon is so pretty."

"Here, let me tie it for you," said the Queen.

So Snow White let the Queen tie the ribbon to her dress. But the Queen tied the ribbon so tightly that Snow White could hardly breathe! She fell to the ground, gasping for breath.

Luckily, the seven dwarfs came home early and saved her by cutting the ribbon away.

The wicked Queen came
back the next day. This time she wore
a different disguise. She tapped on Snow White's
window. "Look, my dear, I have a pretty comb for
you," she called.

Snow White opened the window. "The dwarfs told
me to stay indoors," she said.

"Don't worry," muttered the Queen. "I can place
the comb in your hair from here." So saying, the
Queen placed the comb in Snow White's hair, but the
comb was poisoned. As soon as it touched Snow
White's head, she fell to the ground.

When the dwarfs returned they found Snow
White collapsed on the floor, dying. But the eldest
dwarf saw the strange comb in her hair and grew
suspicious. As soon as he removed the comb, Snow
White quickly recovered.

"The comb was poisoned!" he said.
"You saved my life again," said Snow White,
smiling. "How can I ever thank you all?"

Snow White took one bite from the poisoned half of the apple and fell to the floor as if dead.

The animals went to fetch the dwarfs, who hurried home as fast as they could.

They used all the herbs and medicines they knew to try and cure Snow White. But this time Snow White did not recover. She just lay on the ground, silent and unmoving.

"She's dead," said the eldest dwarf at last.

A great sadness hung over the little cottage.

The seven dwarfs made plans for Snow White's funeral. They were all very upset, but there was work to be done.

They decided that Snow White should be buried in a hilltop garden, which lay among the secret mountains.

The dwarfs made a glass coffin for Snow White and laid her inside. The animals gathered scented flowers to brighten her grave.

On the day of the funeral, the dwarfs set out carrying the glass coffin. It was a long journey. Nevertheless, many animals went along as well, to honour their friend, Snow White.

On the way to the secret mountains, a handsome Prince rode past. When the Prince saw the beautiful Snow White lying in the glass coffin, he asked the dwarfs to stop. The dwarfs were so surprised to meet a Prince, that one of them jumped and dropped the coffin!

The sudden jolt made the piece of poisoned apple fall out of Snow White's throat!

Snow White awoke, as if from a deep sleep. The handsome Prince kissed Princess Snow White's hand. The dwarfs and the animals were so delighted!

What started as a funeral procession, became a wedding between the Prince and the dwarfs' beloved Snow White.

To celebrate, the seven dwarfs brought gifts of gold and silver from their mine in the secret mountains.

The animals came to the wedding bringing fruit and flowers. And Snow White and the Prince had a very happy life together.

As for the wicked Queen… Well, she no longer looked into the magic mirror. All her wicked deeds had made her very ugly indeed!

THE END